Favorite Fairy Tales

Black Beauty

Retold by Rochelle Larkin   **Illustrated by Alan Leiner**

CREATIVE CHILD PRESS

is a registered trademark of Playmore Inc.,
Publishers and Waldman Publishing Corp., New York, N.Y.

Once upon a time I was a young colt, running by my mother's side and learning from her and from the other colts, my friends.

As I grew, I learned to carry a saddle and rider and not to be afraid of other moving things.

I was very proud the day the blacksmith fitted me for my first shoes. It meant that I was ready to work, just like a full grown horse.

A man named Squire Gordon bought me and brought me to his big, clean stable.

It was there that my name, Black Beauty, was given to me by the Squire's wife. She often rode me, while my friend, Ginger, carried the Squire.

One night, during a storm, I was pulling the coach. I didn't want to cross a small bridge with my passengers.

Later we found out the bridge was broken, Squire Gordon and John Manley said I had saved their lives.

Another time, the hotel stable I was in had a dreadful fire. Fortunately, all the horses were saved.

I would have been happy to be with the Gordons all my life, but Mrs. Gordon was sick and the family had to move to a warm climate. It was a sad good-bye for all of us.

I was even sorry to say good-bye to Joe Green, the stable boy, whose neglect had once made me very ill. But it wasn't his fault, really. He just didn't know much about horses then.

My next home was not so happy. A groom rode me too hard on a bad road. My shoe came loose and I had a bad fall.

Then I was sold again. I liked my new master, Jerry Barker. He was a cab driver and we rode together through the streets of a great city.

But he became so sick that a doctor said he must never drive a cab again.

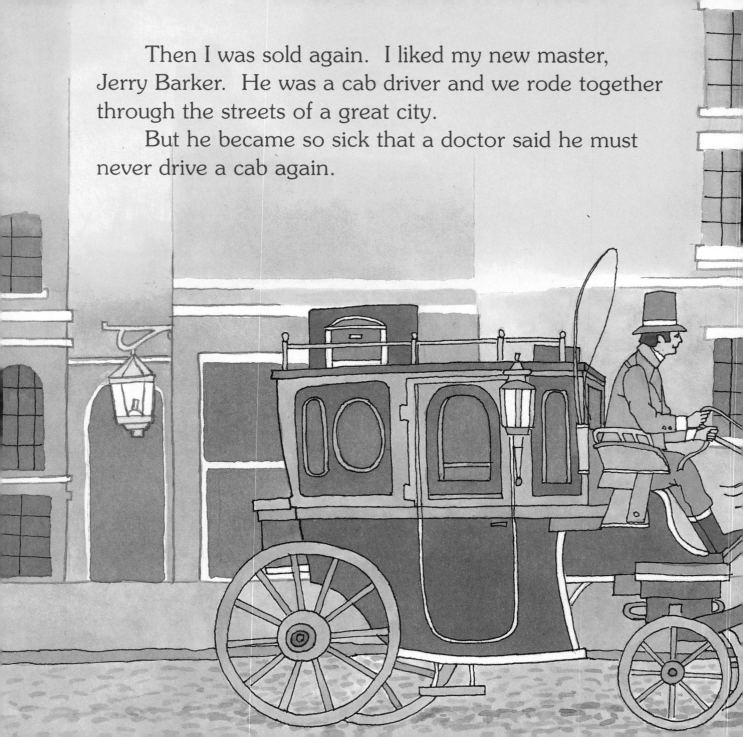

Once more, I lost a good home and a good master.
I was sold again.

Now I had to carry very heavy loads up hill and down hill all day long. If I dared to stop for even a moment, I would feel the sting of a cruel whip.

But all the bad treatment made me weak and ill again. Once more I was to be sold.

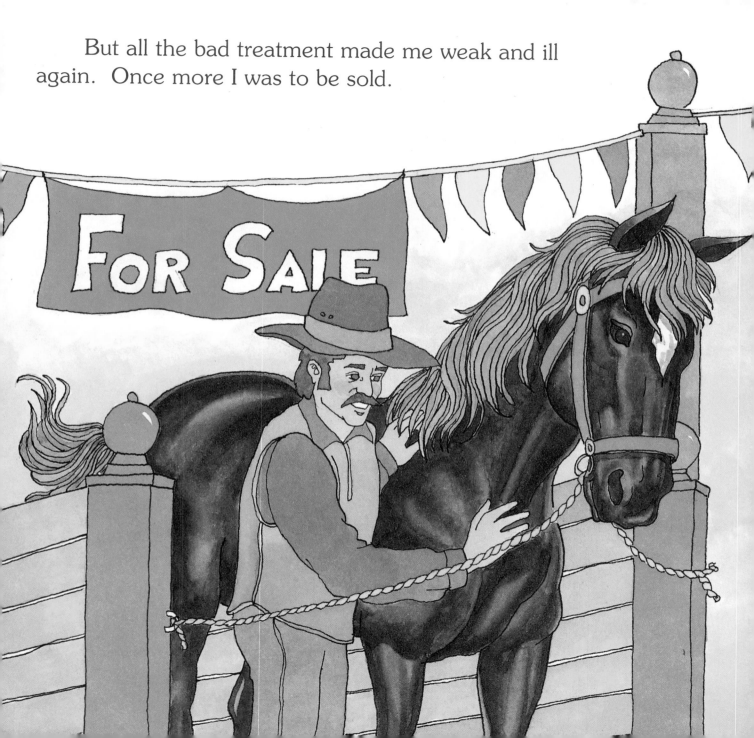

But good fortune was with me again. I was sold to a kindly farmer. Once I was in fresh country air with plentiful food and loving care, I grew strong and healthy.

Now I was sold to two sisters who wanted a quiet, gentle creature for their small cart.

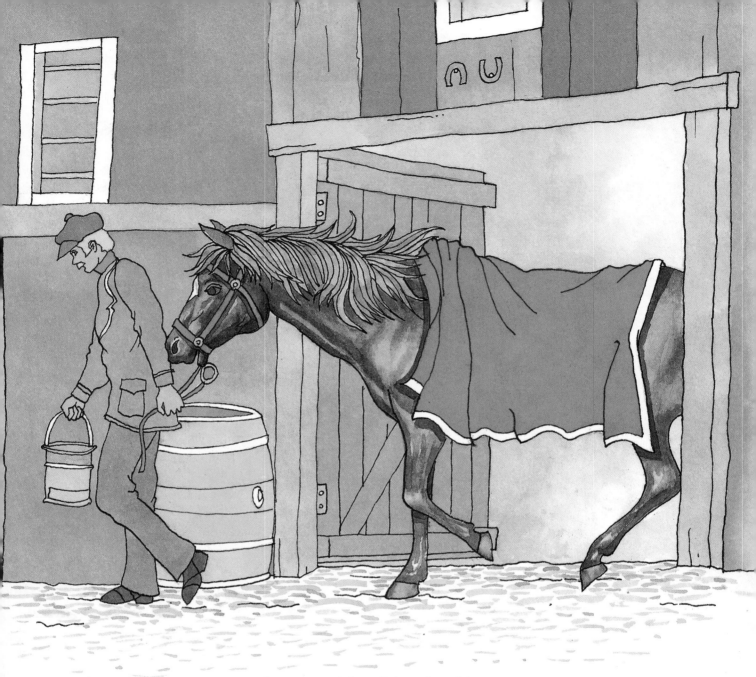

Coming home to their stable, I had a big surprise.

"Black Beauty!" the groom greeted me.

It was Joe Green, whose inexperience at Squire Gordon's so many years before had nearly killed me.

I could tell Joe knew his way around horses now.

He even told the sisters the story of my life at the Gordons. "Black Beauty will never be sold or mistreated again!" they promised.

This is my home now and forever, and I've never been
happier!